FIRST FLIGHT

*FIRST FLIGHT® is an exciting
new series of beginning readers.
The series presents titles which include songs,
poems, adventures, mysteries, and humour
by established authors and illustrators.
FIRST FLIGHT® makes the introduction to
reading fun and satisfying
for the young reader.*

*FIRST FLIGHT® is available in 4 levels
to correspond to reading development.*

Level 1 – Preschool - Grade 1
Large type, repetition of simple concepts that are
perfect for reading aloud, easy vocabulary and
endearing characters in short simple stories for
the earliest reader.

Level 2 – Grade 1 - Grade 3
Longer sentences, higher level of vocabulary,
repetition, and high-interest stories for the
progressing reader.

Level 3 – Grade 2 - Grade 4
Simple stories with more involved plots and a simple
chapter format for the newly independent reader.

Level 4 – Grade 3 - up (First Flight Chapter Books)
More challenging level, minimal illustrations for the
independent reader.

A First Flight® Level Two Reader

Flying Lessons

Celia Godkin

Fitzhenry and Whiteside • Toronto

FIRST FLIGHT® is a registered trademark of Fitzhenry & Whiteside.

First published in the United States in 1999.

Fitzhenry & Whiteside acknowledges with thanks the support of the Government of Canada through its Book Publishing Industry Development Program in the publication of this title.

Printed in Hong Kong.

Design by Wycliffe Smith Design

10 9 8 7 6 5 4 3 2 1

Canadian Cataloguing in Publication Data

Godkin, Celia
Flying lessons

(A first flight level 2 reader)
ISBN 1-55041-401-1 (bound)   ISBN 1-55041-399-6

1. Birds — Juvenile fiction. I. Title. II. Series.

PS8563.O8185F59 1999   jC813'.54   C98-932958-5
PZ7.G5436G1 1999

*For parents
who gave me life,
food, shelter and
flying lessons.*

Mother bird sits on the nest.
There are three sky blue eggs in it.

She sits on them to keep them warm
and dry.

Sometimes father bird sits
on the nest.

Then mother bird
can go catch worms for her supper.

One day an egg moves under mother bird.

She hops to the edge of the nest to see what is happening.

The egg has a crack in it.

A little beak pushes from the inside.
The crack widens.

A little head pushes out through the
crack.

A baby bird struggles free from the
egg.

Soon there are two baby birds in the nest — and one sky-blue egg.

Mother bird throws out the broken egg shells.

Should she throw the egg out too?

No — she sees a crack in it.

A little beak pushes from the inside.
The crack widens.

A little head pushes out through
the crack.

Smallest baby bird struggles free
from the egg.

Now there are three little birds,
and all of them are hungry.

Mother and father
are kept busy
all day long,
feeding their family.

The baby birds eat and grow,
eat and grow, eat and grow.

Soon they are almost as big
as their parents.

Time for their flying lessons!

Mother and father bird show them
what to do.

One by one the baby birds hop out of the nest.

They hop along the branch.

They sit on the branch.

They look down.

The ground is a long, long way down.

Then, one by one, they jump,
open their wings and fly.

Soon they are flying all over
the garden.

But what's this!
Smallest baby bird is still
in the nest.

He won't leave.

He won't take his flying lessons.

Mother bird has to go on
feeding him, right where he is.

Father bird is left to show the other
baby birds how to catch worms.

When the cat enters the garden
father bird cries: "Cheep! Cheep!"

He is telling
the baby birds
that the cat
is coming
to get them.

The baby birds fly away.

The cat is tired
of trying to catch
baby birds that fly away.

He sees that smallest
baby bird is still in the nest.

The cat cannot fly,
but he can climb trees.

He starts to
climb the tree
in which
smallest
baby bird lives.

"Cheep! Cheep!" cries mother bird.

She is telling
smallest
baby bird
that the cat
is coming
to get
him.

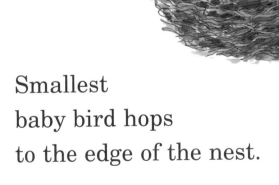

Smallest
baby bird hops
to the edge of the nest.

He can see the cat climbing the tree.
Soon the cat will be on his branch!

Smallest baby bird hops onto the
branch.

He looks down.
The ground is a long, long
way down.

He looks at the cat.

The cat is
very close.

Smallest
baby bird
jumps.

He opens his wings.

He flaps his wings.

He flies!

30

Other Books in the
First Flight® series

Level 1 – **Preschool - Grade 1**
Fishes in the Ocean *written by* Maggee Spicer
and Richard Thompson, *illustrated by* Barbara Hartmann
Then & Now *written by* Richard Thompson, *illustrated*
by Barbara Hartmann

Level 2 – **Grade 1 - Grade 3**
Jingle Bells *written and illustrated by* Maryann Kovalski
Rain, Rain *written and illustrated by* Maryann Kovalski
Omar on Ice *written and illustrated by* Maryann Kovalski

Level 3 – **Grade 2 - Grade 4**
Andrew's Magnificent Mountain of Mittens *written*
by Deanne Lee Bingham *and illustrated by* Kim La Fave
Andrew, Catch That Cat! *written by* Deanne Lee
Bingham, *illustrated by* Kim La Fave

Level 4 – **Grade 3 - up (First Flight Chapter Books)**
The Money Boot *written by* Ginny Russell,
illustrated by John Mardon
Fangs & Me *written by* Rachna Gilmore,
illustrated by Gordon Sauve
More Monsters in School *written by* Martyn Godfrey,
illustrated by John Mardon